W9-AKV-650

Crocodaddy

Crocodaddy

by Kim Norman

illustrated by David Walker

SCHOLASTIC INC.
New York Toronto London Auckland
Sydney Mexico City New Delhi Hong Kong

No part of this publication may be reproduced, stored in a retrieval system, or
transmitted in any form or by any means, electronic, mechanical, photocopying,
recording, or otherwise, without written permission of the publisher. For
information regarding permission, write to Sterling Publishing Co., Inc.,
387 Park Avenue South, New York, NY 10016.

ISBN 978-0-545-24206-6

Text copyright © 2009 by Kim Norman. Illustrations copyright © 2009 by David Walker.
All rights reserved. Published by Scholastic Inc., 557 Broadway, New York, NY 10012,
by arrangement with Sterling Publishing Co., Inc. SCHOLASTIC and associated logos
are trademarks and/or registered trademarks of Scholastic Inc.

12 11 10 9 8 7 6 5 4   11 12 13 14 15/0

Printed in the U.S.A.   40

First Scholastic printing, May 2010

The artwork was prepared using acrylics on heavy paper.
Designed by Scott Piehl and Jessica Dacher

For Kelvin, our own

beloved Crocodaddy.

— K. N.

For our "croc-o-buddies,"

Matthew and Joseph.

— D. W.

Down in the pond by a mossy rock,
something slithers past the dock.
Minnows dart with startled jerks—
this is where the Crocodaddy lurks!

Safe behind the rock, I see
sly old Crocodaddy
smile at me.

Fearlessly, I step in front,
captain of the
Crocodaddy hunt!

Crocodaddy,
Crocodaddy,
swim away fast.
This day's swim
could be your last!

Out on the dock I look below.

Where'd that slippery Crocodaddy go?

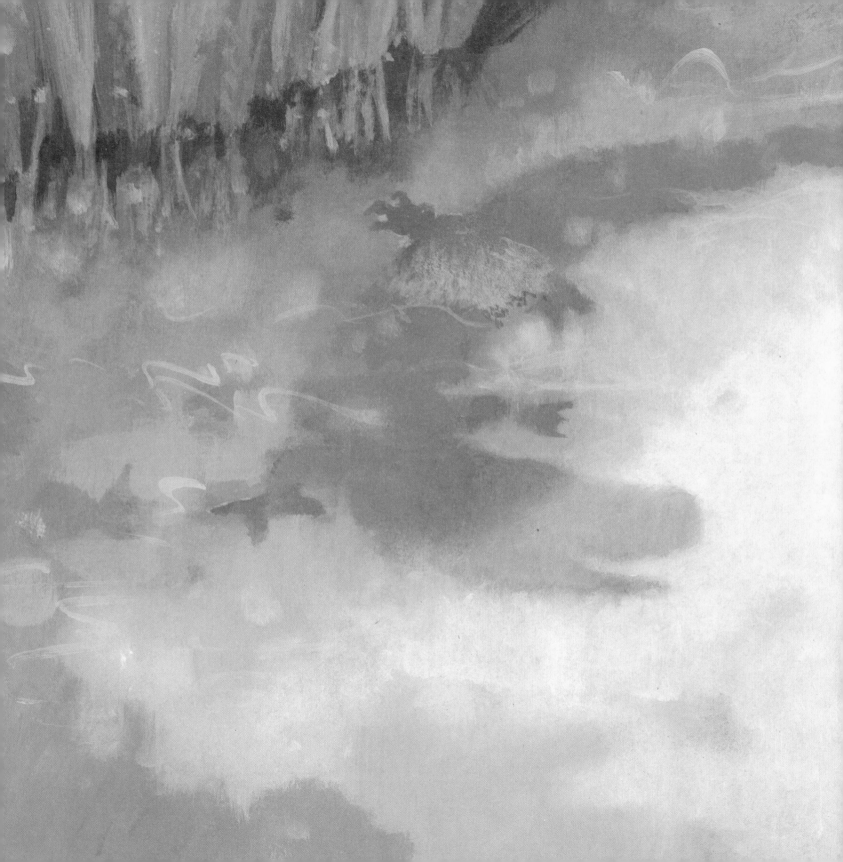

There's his shadow, dark and wet.
I'm gonna tame that Crocodaddy yet!

Tossing off my hat and pack . . . HAAAAH!
I leap on Crocodaddy's back!

Crocodaddy, Crocodaddy,
whatcha gonna do?
Crocodaddy hunter is
RIDING on you!

Water sprays like crystal whips.
Crocodaddy rumbles bubbly lips.
Now he turns his head and winks.

Slowly, s l o w l y, Crocodaddy sinks!

Water rises ripply blue,
chills my laughing belly, too.

Even though he's STILL not tame,
holding tight, I shout his name . . .

Crocodaddy,
Crocodaddy,

can't get away!
I'm on top,
and here I'll stay!

'Round my knees, the water churns.
Splashing, thrashing, Crocodaddy turns,
whips up waves that slap the shore,
then lets out a Crocodaddy...

ROAR!

Such a roar that, oops—oh, no!

SPLASH!

I slip . . . and in I go!

Spitting water, now I see
hunting crocs is hard on ME!

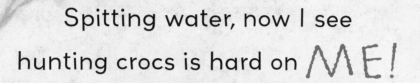

Crocodaddy,
Crocodaddy,

just you wait.
You're gonna bite a
different bait.

Let's just give it one more try.
THIS time when he slithers by,
I discover something new:
Crocodaddy knees are ticklish, too!

THAT'S how you tame a
Crocodaddy pet . . .

(you don't need a rope
and you don't need a net!)

Crocodaddy,
Crocodaddy,
lyin' on the dock—
and I'm a little chip
off the lazy old Croc!